This book belongs

_____

Paperback ISBN: 978-1-63731-401-2
Hardcover ISBN: 978-1-63731-403-6

Printed and bound in the USA.
NinjaLifeHacks.tv

Ninja Life Hacks™

NINJAS
Know the CBT Triangle

Thoughts

By Mary Nhin

Ninja Life Hacks®

Behavior

Feelings

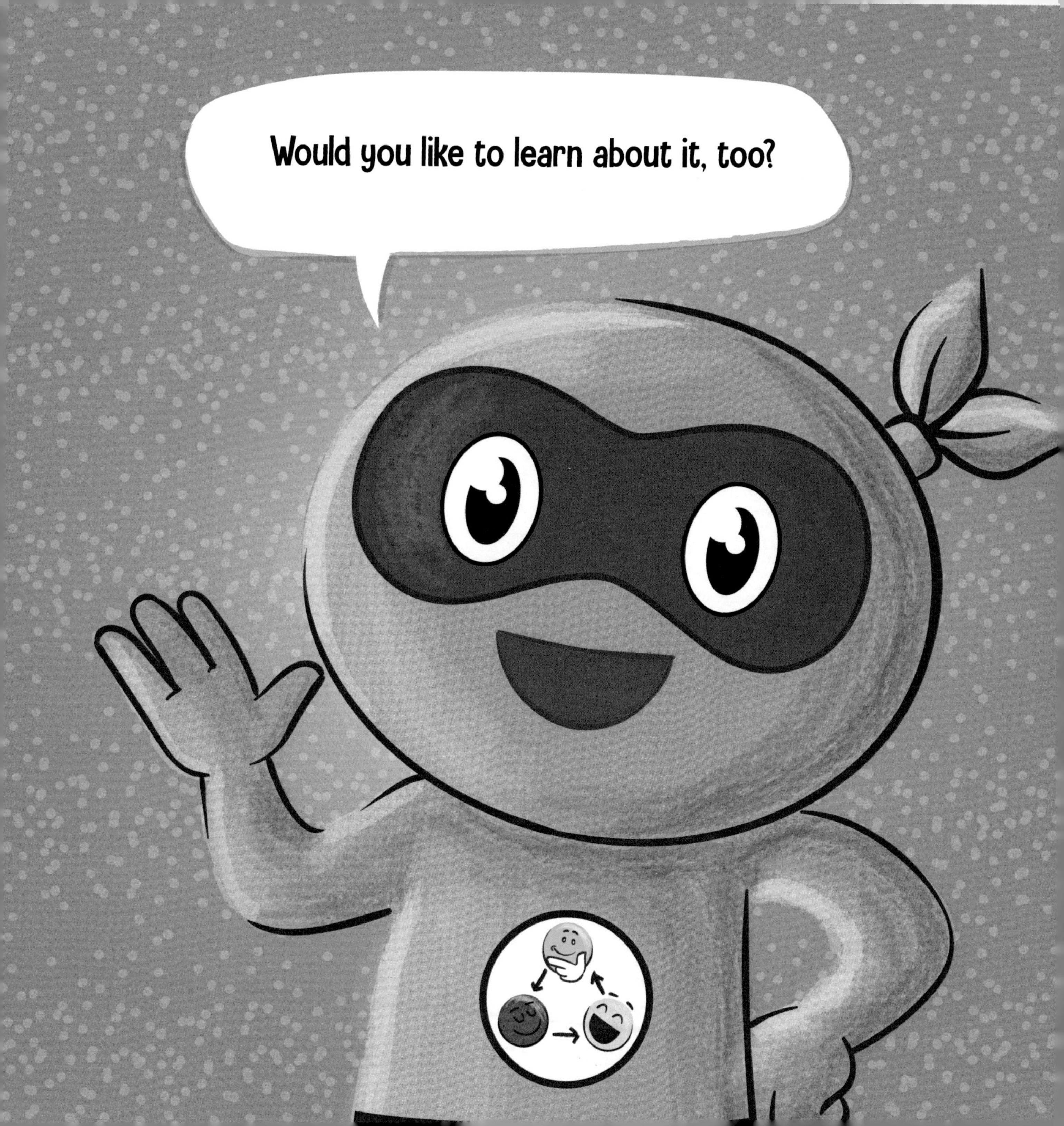
Would you like to learn about it, too?

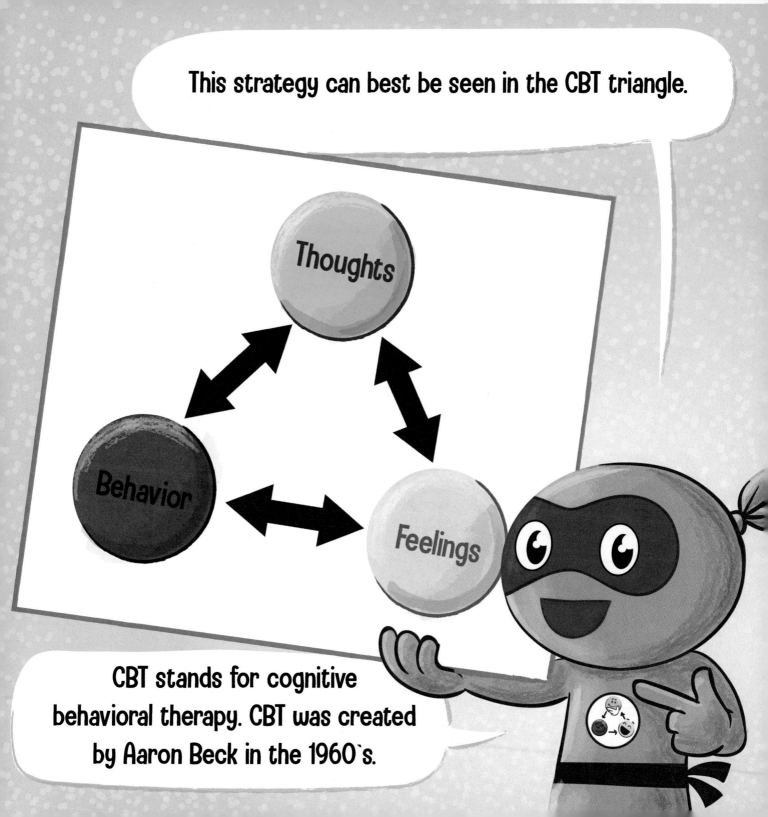

For example, here's what happened to me before I knew about this special superpower:

I woke up feeling nervous and scared. It was the first day of school. My **Thoughts** began:

Today is such a scary day.

I don't know if I'll make any friends.

What if no one likes me?

School is hard.

The chatter in my head wouldn't stop. Have you ever found yourself saying similar things?

Now enter **feelings**. After a morning filled with negative thoughts, I felt even worse. I was extremely anxious and worried about going to school. Overall, I was feeling really bad about myself and the last thing I wanted to do was go to school.

Here comes the **behavior**.

After dragging my feet, I made it out the door and got to school. At school, I didn't talk to anyone and I cried.

Here are some thoughts that help me:

I am capable.

I am smart.

I am worthy.

Mistakes help me learn.

I love to hear from my readers. Email me your feedback or thoughts on what my next story should be at growgritpress@gmail.com

Yours truly, Mary

@marynhin   @GrowGrit
#NinjaLifeHacks

Ninja Life Hacks

Mary Nhin   Ninja Life Hacks

@ninjalifehacks.tv

Made in the USA
Las Vegas, NV
18 March 2024

87397426R00021